Twinkle Twinkle Little Luminous Ball of Gas

and Six More Nerdy Nurse[ry Rhymes]

by Sam and Laura Day

Illustrations by Mike Motz

For Ara

Twinkle Twinkle Little Luminous Ball of Gas

and Six More Nerdy Nursery Rhymes

by Sam and Laura Day

Illustrations by Mike Motz

Twinkle, Twinkle, Little Luminous Ball of Gas

Twinkle, twinkle, little luminous ball of gas.
How I wonder what is your solar mass.
Up above the world so high
Like some crystallized carbon in the sky.
Twinkle, twinkle little luminous ball of gas.
How I wonder what is your solar mass.

$$M_{\odot} = \frac{4\pi^2 \times (1\,AU)^3}{G \times (1\,yr)^2}$$

When the sun's radiation
Is hidden due to the earth's rotation,
Then you show your little photons,
Twinkle, twinkle until you neutron.
Twinkle, twinkle, little luminous ball of gas.
How I wonder what is your solar mass.

5

I'm a Diminutive Kettle

I'm a diminutive kettle, built not to wobble.
Here is my hand grip, here is my nozzle.

Acoustic warning at one hundred C
Tilt halfway then enjoy your tea.

7

Hush Little Human

Hush, little human, don't vibrate your vocal cords,
Mama's gonna buy you a bird of the order Passeriformes.

And if that Mimus polyglottos don't croon,
Mama's gonna buy you a shiny allotrope of carbon.

9

And if that allotrope of carbon turns
to a zinc and copper, yellow fusion,
Mama's gonna buy you a reflective surface
with no visual occlusions.

And if that amorphous solid structure gets broke,
Mama's gonna acquire you a billy goat.

And if that bovid won't draw an object with sufficient force,
Mama's gonna buy you a cart
and an adult male of the species Bos Taurus.

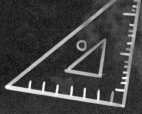

And if that bullock cart flips one eighty degrees,
Mama's gonna buy you a canine named DeeOhGee.

13

And if that canine named DeeOhGee won't vocalize,
Mama's gonna buy you a stallion to mobilize.

And if that stallion gets a leg twisted,
You'll still be the most agreeable baby in the solar system.

Mary Had a Ruminant

Mary had a ruminant,
Even-toed ungulate,
Mary had a baby sheep
Whose fleece appeared to reflect all of the wavelengths
of the visible spectrum comparably to
atmospheric water vapor frozen into hexagonal ice crystals

120°W

40°N

N
E
W
S

And to each latitudinal longitudinal coordinate
that Mary went,
Mary went, Mary went,
Each latitudinal longitudinal coordinate that Mary went
The lamb had a one hundred percent probability to go.

He followed her to the educational institution one day,
educational institution one day,
educational institution one day.
He followed her to the educational institution one day
Which was contrary to the established regulations.

It made the children have an audible physiological response to the humor and play,
audible physiological response to the humor and play
It made the children have an audible physiological response to the humor and play
To see a lamb at the educational institution.

19

Three Vermin with No Retinas

Three vermin with no retinas,
Three vermin with no retinas!
Observe their behavior,
Observe their behavior!

They chased the farmer's spouse because
She severed them up to the torso fuzz.
What a unique and singular sight it was
Three vermin with no retinas!

The Lilliputian Arachnid

The Lilliputian arachnid
ascended the gutter drain.
Precipitation gathered
and flushed her back again.

The cumulonimbi parted
and H_2O evaporated
and the miniscule arachnid
and the drain got reacquainted.

23

Rock-a-bye Infant

Rock-a-bye infant, in the flora canopy.
When air masses move,
The cradle will swing

When the branch splits,
They'll drop from the tree.
The infant's first lesson
In gravity.

Meet Sam and Laura Day

Sam and Laura Day are a husband and wife writing duo. Laura is a lab scientist, bread baker, and amateur barber. Sam is a software development manager, invention convention winner, and miniature golf enthusiast. They live with their daughter and imaginary pet cat named Pistachio Mustachio.